Ellie's Shoes

For Ellie Spens

A Red Fox Book

Published by Random House Children's Books
20 Vauxhall Bridge Road, London SW1V 2SA

A division of The Random House Group Ltd
London Melbourne Sydney Auckland
Johannesburg and agencies throughout the world

Copyright © Sarah Garland 1997

1 3 5 7 9 10 8 6 4 2

First published in Great Britain by
The Bodley Head Children's Books 1997
Red Fox edition 2001

Printed in Hong Kong by Midas Printing Ltd

THE RANDOM HOUSE GROUP Limited Reg. No. 954009

www.randomhouse.co.uk

ISBN 0 09 969251 1

Ellie's Shoes

Sarah Garland

RED FOX

Mum!

Where's your vest, Ellie?

And your shorts, Ellie?

Now where did you put your shoes?

In the bin?

On the chair?

Beside the cat?

Under the bed?

Where are those shoes?

Ellie's shoes are...

in the box!

One shoe,

two shoes,

Ellie's dressed!